WELSH
MONSTERS
&
MYTHICAL
BEASTS

Welsh Monsters & Mythical Beasts:
A Guide to the Legendary Creatures from Celtic-Welsh Myth and Legend

Published by Eye of Newt Books Inc. • www.eyeofnewtpress.com
Eye of Newt Books Inc. 56 Edith Drive, Toronto, Ontario, M4R 1C3

First edition edited & published by C.C.J. Ellis, 2019;
Second edition edited & published by Eye of Newt Books Inc., 2021

Design and layout copyright © 2021 C.C.J. Ellis
Text copyright © 2021 C.C.J. Ellis
Illustrations by C.C.J. Ellis copyright © 2021 Eye of Newt Books Inc.

ISBN: 9781777081775

Printed in China

—

Library and Archives Canada Cataloguing in Publication

Title: Welsh Monsters & Mythical Beasts
Subtitle: A Guide to the Legendary Creatures from Celtic-Welsh Myth and Legend
Other titles: Welsh monsters & mythical beasts | Welsh monsters and mythical beasts
Names: Ellis, C. C. J., author, illustrator.
Description: The second edition.
Identifiers: Canadiana 20210263768 | ISBN 9781777081775 (hardcover)
Subjects: LCSH: Mythology, Welsh. | LCSH: Folklore—Wales. | LCSH: Monsters—Wales. |
LCSH: Animals— Folklore.
Classification: LCC GR150 .E45 2021 | DDC 398.209429/0454—dc23

WRITTEN & ILLUSTRATED
BY C.C.J. ELLIS

WELSH
MONSTERS
&
MYTHICAL
BEASTS

A GUIDE TO THE LEGENDARY CREATURES
FROM CELTIC-WELSH MYTH AND LEGEND

WOOL OF BAT

a series from
EYE OF NEWT
BOOKS

THIS BOOK IS DEDICATED TO:

The Ellis family
for all their love and support which helped
make this book possible.

Yadzia Williams and Steve Kegan
for believing in me and where my art could take me.

WELSH MONSTERS

My first thought upon seeing *Welsh Monsters* was
"Goodness, what a useful book!" If that adjective sounds a little staid
and uninspired, let me elucidate.

U for Unexpected. I did not realize, though it makes perfect sense, that
there were so many astonishing creatures in Welsh legend.

S for Serendipitous. Encountering the intricacies of the genesis and
syncretism of myth, and the originality of the creatures inhabiting the
wild spaces of the Welsh mind.

E for Exotic. The names of the creatures themselves are fantastical,
and are already a journey in themselves.

F for Fascinating. Half-familiar (they do have aspects in common with
other fantastical denizens of the British Isles, but we are clearly in
another world) but nevertheless doubly otherworldly.

U for Understandable. The book is well constructed, clear, and legible,
a must for any guide, especially a guide to the fantastic.

L for Lovely (just plain) …

See? Very USEFUL. A must-have guide to those
creatures you hope never to encounter except in story
and imagination.

— JOHN HOWE

TABLE of CONTENTS

FOREWORD
By Stephanie Law

Folklore and mythology had their place in bygone eras as a way of connecting humans to the world around us. So much of the inner workings of nature was beyond our understanding. So much was a mystery, from the refraction of light into a rainbow, to the shifting of tectonic plates in an earthquake, to nebulous things like the dark shadows of a forest. In order to deal with these unknowns, we used our gift of imagination and storytelling, harnessing miracles and terrors into wonders and anthropomorphized beings. A rainbow became a bridge between the realms of mortals and gods, an earthquake explained as the thrashings of an enchained beast, the dark forest haunted by spirits and shape-changers alternately offering gifts and curses to passersby.

You would think that science would dissolve the reality of these old myths, replacing awe with practicality, and yet the stories still persist. The creatures that our ancestors created and told tales about around their hearth fires still have life in a modern age.

Knowing that the moon is a satellite orbiting the Earth hundreds of thousands of miles away and that the shapes and shadows we see on its face are craters and mountains and icecaps, while at the same time sitting with my family during Mid-Autumn Festival in September and eating our mooncakes as we gaze at the full moon and tell tales of the rabbit who pounds away at a mortar and pestle to create pills of immortality: this is magic. We can hold these two realities in our mind simultaneously—the moon as we understand and know it to be, as well as all the weight of wonder and awe and reverence it has been imbued with by the stories of my own Chinese culture and any other culture that has ever turned eyes to the gleaming white companion in the sky. In remembering the mythology of the moon, we share for a moment what every human who has stood on a dark hillside and gazed skyward has ever felt.

Artwork to right: *Ancient* by Stephanie Law

That is the gift that Ellis offers you with this beautiful collection of Welsh creatures and their stories. In sinuous lines and vibrant watercolours, they illustrate a forgotten world. In a time when we are sometimes so inundated with information and pop culture that borrows from, while obscuring, the original mythological sources, it is more important than ever to dive into the tales in their original forms, because these are our ties to a past where magic exists. In holding this knowledge in your mind concurrent with our contemporary context, it makes our whole existence that of wonder and magic.

After sifting through these pages, perhaps you will think about gwibers next time you are hiking around a reservoir, see the shadow of their scales in the reflections on the water's surface, or hear the Hounds of Annwn on the wail of a wind. Maybe you'll be lucky enough to catch a glimpse of a pwca from the corner of your eye. Ellis has given new life to these and dozens of other creatures, in all their glory of scales and feathers, claws and crests.

Stephanie Law

INTRODUCTION
By Sian Powell

Human beings have always crafted, shared, and adapted stories of fantastical creatures and monsters. Sometimes we share stories that are intended to scare, to keep children away from those hidden, beguiling places where they might find themselves in danger, were they ever to venture there alone. Sometimes we share stories to explain and rationalize things that are a mystery to us. These stories can help us make sense of strange phenomena, like lights over the moors, unfamiliar shapes in the trees, disappearances of neighbours, and the sounds heard alone in the forest that make your hair stand on end.

And then there are the stories of creatures that have evolved so many times since their genesis that they have become different beasts entirely. Local folk heroes battling giants become Christian saints besting the devil. This is one of the things that I love most about folklore, mythology, and legends. We are always changing the stories we tell, emphasizing the parts that fascinate us and discarding those that don't. There should never be a "correct" version of a story or a single description of a monster. To some people, a fairy is a sweet, benevolent creature with glittering wings and a tiny magical wand. To others, a fairy is something to be frightened of, a creature from another world to respect, and if at all possible, avoid.

Folklore is a fascinating historical tool that helps us understand the people of the past while continuing to inspire the people of today. However, as important as it is to perform and to write stories, one of the greatest ways to preserve the stories of mythological creatures is to visualize them. Ellis has presented a range of creatures, both regional and national, in this beautifully illustrated collection. These images bring the folklore of Wales to vibrant, wonderful life for an audience within and without Wales. It is fair to say that not everyone is interested in the academic discipline of combing through dusty old tomes to find information. This book offers everyone a glimpse of the magical cultural heritage and tradition of storytelling in Wales.

Wales has a rich tapestry of folkloric creatures, but it is difficult to find visual representations outside of the same few pictures that have been used and reused on countless folklore webpages.

Ellis's inclusion of so many new artistic representations of mythological creatures is a gift to any storyteller, because it is the image of the monster that we hope to conjure up when we tell stories around a fire, to a friend or family member.

One of my favourite things about folklore is that similar stories and creatures can be found in various cultures across the world. This is proof to me that human beings are all linked by a key motivation, storytelling and the oral tradition, no matter where we are from. But for all that beauty in similarity, there is also the danger of loss if we do not celebrate some of the differences too. If we did not acknowledge the regional variations of fairies, water horses, and dragons, then we may be in jeopardy of losing the vital connections to the local landscapes that are the backdrops of these stories. There is also a possible erosion of language; if the mythological creatures in this book were not given their Welsh names, then all the history and intricacy of their origins might be lost. When the Cŵn Annwn become the Hounds of Hell, there is no connection to their hunting with Arawn, King of the Otherworld.

The inclusion of the Welsh names and their respective pronunciations should not be seen as exclusionary to others around the world, who may know of similar creatures with different names. The use of Welsh is a celebration of the stories that have been told in Wales and an invitation to keep sharing them. Storytelling has always played a significant role in the culture of Wales, whether in singing, poetry, or folk stories. The *Mabinogion*, which is the source of many of the creatures collected here, is a collection of some of the oldest pieces of prose literature in Britain. These written stories were almost certainly adapted from earlier oral performances and include some examples of Welsh poetic forms, such as the englyn, within them.

This is all to say that Ellis has joined many historians, authors, artists, and musicians in continuing a long tradition of storytelling within Wales. I hope that people will read these descriptions, memorize these images, and create their own stories in the same way that Ellis has read and been inspired by the *Mabinogion*, Arthurian literature, and local folklore.

I know that I'm already dreaming of a world where innkeepers polish their best silver dishes when the mountain fairies take shelter, where brothers visit their fairy mother in her watery home, where the soft barking of hounds means the Cŵn Annwn, or wild hunt, is nearby… This collection of "monsters" is a wonderful love letter to Wales and to Welsh mythology.

AUTHOR'S WELSH LANGUAGE GUIDE

*"Welsh is of this soil, this island, the senior language of the men
of Britain; and Welsh is beautiful."*

– J.R.R. Tolkien

In addition to my endeavour to preserve and share these fantastical creatures from Welsh mythology, I also wish to share with you my native tongue. Cymraeg,[1] or Welsh, as it is known in English, is a language with ancient British roots and is considered one of the oldest languages in Europe.

Due to the Laws in Wales Acts 1535 and 1542, the use of the Welsh language was largely banned in public office, as these laws removed its status as an official language. Thankfully, valiant efforts and political campaigns brought it back from the brink of extinction, and in 1992 the Welsh Language Bill was passed, giving the language equal status with English in all public spaces in Wales. Today in some areas it is people's first language and is taught in schools. There are also Welsh language TV channels, radio shows, films, books, and annual festivals. Although Welsh is now spoken by many people throughout Wales it is still considered an endangered language, which is why I feel it important to provide a brief introduction in this book.

Throughout the text I have provided a pronunciation guide for the Welsh words featured. It is important to me that the Welsh terms be honoured, but also that you, the reader, might try to read and speak them. The following are a few notes that I hope can guide you through the pronunciations given throughout the book. Remember that Welsh has a natural beauty and flow and has even inspired the likes of J.R.R. Tolkien, featuring prominently in his fictional Elvish language, Sindarin. So, keep the fair folk in mind when you attempt these ancient words.

1   kym-rah-egg

- "au" sounds like "eye"
- "c" is almost always hard, like "k"
- "ch" in Welsh is a back of the throat sound, not "ch" as in "chair" or "chasm" but rather like "kh," like the Hebrew letter "chet"
- "dd" is often pronounced like a "th" unless it is at the beginning of a word
- "f" is often pronounced as a "v"
- "ll" is special in Welsh. It involves a flick of the tongue against the front teeth creating a "thl" sort of sound. This is a rule that is only mostly true; the few exceptions in this text are noted.
- "r" should be rolled in Welsh, especially if it is found at the end of a word
- "y" means "The" and sounds like "eh" or "uh"

AN INTRODUCTION TO WALES

There exists a land of rolling green hills, dark forests, rugged coastlines, and dramatic mountains. It is the country of Wales, snugly situated within the British Isles. It is bordered on the east by England, and on the west side by the Irish Sea.

Wales is regarded as a modern Celtic nation, its national identity mainly consisting of Celtic Britons. Wales is culturally unique within the British Isles as a bilingual country wherein the population is fluent in both English and Welsh. Cardiff, the capital of Wales, sits on the south coast and the national flag comprises a red dragon on a green and white background.

Famous for its vast woodlands, you can find the breathtaking Snowdonia National Park in the North, the rolling Brecon Beacons in the South, and the dramatic Pembrokeshire National Parks along the southwest coast. Wales is steeped in ancient mythology and history, renowned for its culture and medieval past; today you can find many ancient castles, barrows, standing stones, and earth works all across the country.

One of Wales' most notable literary compositions is the *Mabinogion* or *Mabinogi*,[1] one of the earliest pieces of prose in Britain. Consisting of several written works, ancient poems, and medieval manuscripts, most notably the *White Book of Rhydderch* or *Llyfr Gwyn Rhydderch*[2] and the *Red Book of Hergest* or *Llyfr Coch Hergest*.[3] The *Mabinogion* tells tales of Culhwch[4] and Olwen, King Arthur, and many more mythological figures. These stories were compiled at some point during the twelfth and thirteenth centuries and, to this day, still feature in popular media around the world.

---

1   mah-ben-og-eon OR mah-ben-ogee

2   thl-ee-ver gw-in rhyth-air-ch

3   thl-ee-ver coa-kh her-guest

4   keel-hoo-kh

THE ANNWN
Celtic Underworld

The Annwn,[1] or Otherworld, is a magical realm, which is home to a host of magical creatures and spirits; it is a place of eternal youth, there is no sickness or disease, and there is often an abundance of food.

Annwn features prominently within Arthurian legend and is referenced frequently in the stories of the *Mabinogion* and in several Irish myths. It is within the first branch of the *Mabinogion* that the Annwn is referred to the most. According to legend, the world's appearance is strikingly similar to our own world; it's believed to exist parallel to our reality, only occasionally intruding into our plane of existence. It plays a large role in many Celtic legends, with humans often stumbling into it by mistake or being invited in by one of the beings that lives there. A transference to the Annwn is often signalled by sudden lack of wind, an eerie silence, the onset of a sudden thick fog, or the appearance of unusual animals that glow with a supernatural light.

Time runs quite differently in the Annwn: spending up to three weeks in this magical plane could mean spending up to three years in our time. Often those who are lured to the Otherworld by its inhabitants eventually return to find their world changed, their friends and family long passed.

Its exact location remains a mystery and transference into the Annwn is often random; however, it can be reached on a particular island off the west coast of Wales, through underground tunnels close to ancient burial mounds, and through deep underground caves.

Avalon, a place referenced in Arthurian legend is sometimes considered to be an island situated within the Annwn, known as the island of Afallach,[2] where King Arthur himself when mortally injured was taken to heal.

1   ah-noon
2   ava-thl-akh

DREIGIAU

Dragons

AFANC
Lake Monster

Once considered a water god by the people of Wales, afanc[1] are reptilian water dragons similar to the Loch Ness Monster. They resemble enormous crocodiles with long coiling bodies covered in impenetrable scales, making them almost impossible to kill. Afanc dwell in freshwater lakes and flooded caves. Fish are their main source of food, but they have been known to eat livestock and people that wander too close to their lakes by coiling around them, crushing them, and swallowing them whole.

There have been reports of afanc spotted numerous times in Glaslyn Lake, which is believed by locals to be bottomless. In Llyn-y-Gadair[2] Lake in Snowdonia a swimmer was said to have been dragged into the depths by an afanc's armoured coils.

THE AFANC OF CONWY:

In North Wales the inhabitants of Conwy[3] were regularly plagued with terrible floods that drowned their livestock and ruined their crops. The cause of this destruction was an afanc that had grown too large for the lake in which it resided. This particular afanc was so enormous and strong it could break the banks of its lake, causing regular floods. The people of Conwy devised a plan to move the creature. Afanc have a fondness for music and so the daughter of a local farmer lured it from the lake with her song; the creature swam towards her and fell asleep with its head on her lap.

The local men then emerged from their hiding places, bound the Afanc with iron chains and, with the help of several oxen, dragged it to Ffynnon Las[4] or Lake of the Blue Fountain, close to the summit of Snowdon, where they released it, and where it has resided ever since.

1	av-ank
2	th-l in ugh gad-aye-er
3	kon-wee
4	fun-on lass

CEILIOG NEIDR

Cockatrice

Ceiliog neidr,[1] the Welsh cockatrice, is akin to the form of a bird or raptor, with the males having chicken-like wattles, horns on the top of their heads, and bright impressive plumage used to attract potential mates. Like its larger cousin, the basilisk, the ceiliog neidr is able to kill or paralyze its prey through eye contact. If that isn't enough this terrifying creature secretes a poison from its skin and spits acid. It preys on smaller animals like mice, rabbits, and birds, and has a habit of decimating chicken flocks.

Cockatrice are exceptionally territorial creatures; should one meet another they will fight to the death. They are not the brightest of creatures and will even fight their own reflections until they die of exhaustion.

Weasels and ferrets are the only known animals that are immune to the ceiliog neidr's death-glare; they were often kept as pets to keep cockatrices at bay and away from livestock.

THE COCKATRICE OF CASTLE GWYS:

There was once a cockatrice that dwelled on the grounds of Castle Gwys,[2] Pembrokeshire. This cockatrice had multiple eyes, which made it near impossible for anyone to sneak up on it; as far as the story goes this particular creature was harmless and would run away when approached.

1   kay-lee-og nay-dare

2   gw-is

DRAIG GOCH
Red Dragon

Perhaps the most famous creature in all of Wales, featured on the national flag, draig goch[1] is an important symbol of Welsh culture. The sighting of a dragon is often associated with the coming of royalty or King Arthur, whose father was named Uther Pendragon, meaning "dragon's head."

Draig goch are fairly small compared to other species of dragon. They are often depicted with four legs and a pair of bat-like wings capable of long-distance sustained flight; however, there have been many artworks of creatures with just two back legs and a pair of wings, more akin to a wyvern but easily mistaken for a dragon. Draig goch are magnificent beasts that can range from bright red or copper in colour to a glistening metallic gold, and have the ability to camouflage into their environment. Their scales are thick and water-resistant, allowing the rain to simply roll off their backs.

A red dragon's tongue is long and barbed like a cat's and they are sometimes depicted with cow-like ears and a pointed nose. A sharp spine or arrowhead-shaped club can be found on the end of their tails; they have a habit of hissing and striking with their tails to ward off would-be dragon slayers.

These large dragons can be found at high altitudes, preferring to live in mountain caves close to springs or river sources. Like most dragons they are very fond of shiny objects, and often keep a hoard in their lair to impress a potential mate.

Welsh red dragons prefer to ambush their prey, dulling their colour to blend into the surroundings and striking when an unsuspecting sheep, mountain goat, or wild pony wanders too close. These dragons are capable of breathing fire, often choosing to cook their meat before eating it.

1   dr-eye-g go-kh

THE DRAGONS OF DINAS EMRYS

Dinas Emrys,[1] or the fortress of Ambrosius, is a rocky outcrop near Beddgelert[2] in North Wales. According to legend, King Vortigern fled to Wales to escape Anglo-Saxon invaders. He started to build a fort on the rocks; however, every morning he would return to find the masonry collapsed in a heap. This continued for some time until Vortigern sought the help of a young boy named Myrddin,[3] also known as Merlin.

At first Vortigern planned on sacrificing the boy to appease the restless mountain. Myrddin, on the other hand, proposed that instead they should investigate in case something under the mountain was causing the tremors. They discovered a pair of fighting dragons, one red and one white, who had been causing the masonry to collapse. The dragons, having been disturbed, rushed from the mountain and continued their battle in the sky. The white dragon seemed to have the upper hand as it drove its opponent to the ground. The red dragon kept fighting ferociously, eventually causing the white dragon to retreat and fly away.

1   dee-nahs em-rees
2   bethe-ghel-ert
26 3   murth-een

GWIBER
Flying Viper

Today the Welsh word "gwiber"[1] translates to "adder," a type of snake native to the British Isles, but many centuries ago the word referred to a "flying viper."

These winged serpents are often described as brightly coloured with large glistening wings and distinctive markings. They have long snake-like bodies covered with tough scales, sharp spines, and the largest reach up to twenty-four feet in length. Ancient gwiberod[2] were reputed to reach up to forty feet in length! They move by slithering or gliding from place to place. Long retractable fangs can deliver a potent venom, killing their victims in minutes.

Often found in dark, dank caves, woodlands, and swamps, gwiberod prefer to live near water where the humidity is high. They prefer freshwater rivers and lakes with plenty of foliage to hide in, preying on fish, sheep, goats, and anyone foolish enough to stray too close to their lairs. There are reports of winged serpents across Wales; in Glamorgan,[3] winged serpents are believed to inhabit the woods near Penllin[4] castle, Penmark, and around the outskirts of the town of Cowbridge, where there are numerous reports and sightings of flying snakes.

According to locals the gwiberod developed a taste for chickens and livestock, and have even attacked passersby if they strayed too close, beating them with their wings and whipping them with their long tails. To this day there are people who claim that these pesky creatures exist, but were driven into hiding by the loud sounds of aircraft coming from Cardiff International Airport.

1   gwee-bair

2   gwee-bair-odd

3   gla-mor-gan

4   pen-thlean

THE GWIBER OF PENMACHNO

There was once a gwiber that lived in the Welsh valley of Penmachno,[1] terrorizing inhabitants and anyone foolish enough to stray near to its lair. The local residents offered a large reward to anyone who could kill the beast, and a young man named Owen took up the challenge. He consulted a local wise man to divine his chances of success and the wise man told him that the creature would bite him.

The next day, in disguise, Owen returned to the wise man to once again divine the future. The wise man told him bluntly that he would fall and suffer a broken neck. Owen paid a third and final visit, this time using another disguise. Again, the wise man told him bluntly that he would not succeed and that this time he would drown.

Believing the wise man to be a fraud, Owen fearlessly set off down into the valley to kill the gwiber. The valley was steep and slippery; whilst Owen stood on a rocky ledge the gwiber suddenly swooped down and bit him on the neck. Owen lashed out with his sword but slipped and fell from the ledge. As he fell, he smashed into the rocks, snapping his neck like a twig before plunging into the river far below where he drowned.

1   pen-makh-no

BWYSTFILOD

Beasts

ADAR LLWCH GWIN

Griffin

According to Welsh legend, the adar llwch gwin[1] are giant, white, bird-like bwystfilod,[2] or beasts, similar to griffins; they have enormous shining talons on each foot, long pointed ears, piercing jewel-like eyes ranging from golden to red, and enormous feathery wings with a span of twenty-five to thirty feet. They are also remarkably skilled mimics, replicating animal calls and even human speech like a parrot.

These intelligent beasts are incredibly loyal and protective so were often kept as pets, even being ridden into battle by the warrior Drudwas ap Tryffin.[3] However, they also have a habit of taking commands too literally. One such example was when Drudwas commanded them to kill the first person to enter the field of battle against King Arthur. However, Arthur was delayed and Drudwas made the first move, so his adar llwch gwin turned on him and tore him apart.

Sadly, there are no recent tales of this stunningly beautiful Welsh beast, but the name aderyn[4] llwch gwin was later used to describe different species of raptor, like falcons and hawks. It is also a complimentary phrase used to describe a brave young man.

1   ad-ar thloo-kh gween

2   boo-ist veal-odd

3   drid-wahs ap trugh-fin

      4   ah-dare-in

CATH PALUG
Palug's Cat

In Welsh legend, Cath Palug,[1] or Palug's cat, is a monstrous cat the size of a horse with razor-sharp claws and glowing yellow eyes.

The stories of Cath Palug's origins vary: some say it was a mysterious kitten rescued from the sea off Anglesey,[2] or that it was the spawn of a goblin, whilst others believed it was a demon birthed by a cow or swine. Regardless of where it came from, this gigantic cat became a plague upon the Isle of Anglesey. It is even described in Arthurian legend as killing over 180 warriors who attempted to slay it. According to this legend, it was Arthur himself who eventually slew the beast and ended its reign of terror.

1   kath palg, the "g" is hard, as in "good"
2   angle-sea

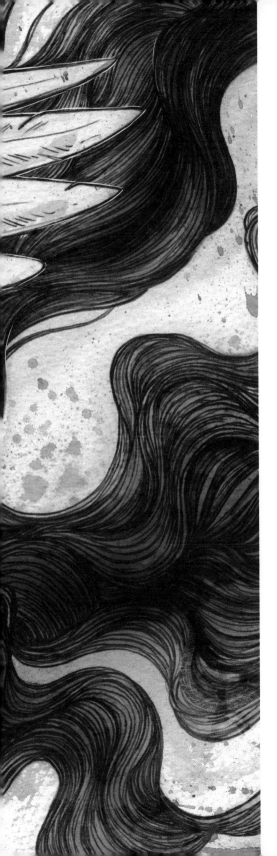

CEFFYL DŴR
Water Horse

Believed to be a cousin of the Scottish kelpie, the ceffyl dŵr[1] is a type of water spirit. They are said to lure travellers off the safety of the path, causing them to get lost.

The legend of the ceffyl dŵr varies depending on the region of Wales it is from. In North Wales, it is said that the creature entices people to ride it before proceeding to fly up into the sky and dropping the rider to their death. In South Wales, ceffylau dŵr[2] are seen in a more positive light, being described as luminous in appearance with beautiful wings.

Unlike the swamp-dwelling kelpie, ceffyl dŵr are said to inhabit freshwater lakes, mountain pools, and waterfalls. They also have large feathery wings that appear at will.

These creatures can evaporate into a fine mist when startled and are highly territorial; they have been known to trample travellers who wander too close to their young.

1   keff-ill do-wer
2   keff-ugh-lie do-wer

CŴN ANNWN
Hounds of Annwn

Cŵn Annwn[1] are spectral white hounds with bright red ears and glowing eyes. They are large, unnaturally fast dogs with long legs and slim muscular builds. Their bark seems loud when they are at a distance and as they approach their bark appears softer. They can sometimes be found gathering around graveyards and mass burial grounds, or running in packs during the autumn, winter, and early spring months.

Often owned by Celtic gods and inhabitants of the Otherworld, Cŵn Annwn (also known as Dogs of the Sky) are associated with death and the wild hunt. They are believed to escort souls on their journeys to and from the Otherworld.

As Christianity spread across Europe, these otherworldly beasts became known as the Hounds of Hell and it was believed by many that they were the pets of Satan himself.

Arawn,[2] King of the Annwn, owned a pack of several hounds; these creatures are referenced in the first branch of the *Mabinogion,* which details the hounds taking down and feasting on a white stag.

1   koon an-noon

2   arr-ah-oon

GWYLLGI
Twilight Dog

Also known as the Dark Dog or Twilight Dog, the Gwyllgi[1] is a monstrous black canid that stalks travellers. It has red glowing eyes and a fiery gaze which renders victims paralyzed.

Like many black dog legends, the Gwyllgi is a huge and stocky creature like a wolf or mastiff. Its fur is normally jet black, thick and shaggy in texture, and it has pointed ears and incredibly long teeth and claws. It has a fondness for human flesh, often stalking its victim for days or weeks before finally attacking.

To this day, there are still many reported sightings of this fearsome creature in North Wales, particularly in Nant y Garth[2] pass near Denbighshire, Marchwiel[3] in Wrecsham,[4] and on the Isle of Anglesey.

The Gwyllgi might be seen at night wandering through thick forest and has been spotted patrolling graveyards and castle grounds.

1   gwee-thl-gee
2   nant uh garth
3   marc-kh-wheel
4   rex-am

LLAMHIGYN Y DŴR
The Water Leaper

Llamhigyn y dŵr,[1] the Welsh water leaper, is a creature that can be best described as a large frog or toad with bat-like wings and horns. It is normally dark brown or green in colour and its back is covered in rows of sharp spines. The adolescents have long lizard-like tails, which, like their frog cousins', will drop off once they reach adulthood.

Don't be fooled by their cute appearance; they are innovative little critters and have learned to snap fishing lines so they can make off with someone's catch; they have also learned to steal food from humans so don't be surprised if they steal a sandwich or two from your lunch box. Llamhigyn y dŵr is also very fond of collecting shiny objects like crystals, seashells, and pebbles, and some have been observed attaching these items to their backs to act as camouflage or to impress a potential mate.

They can be found in fresh- or saltwater swamps, lakes, pools, and caves, often seen gliding across the water catching insects and fish. Their regular food source isn't limited to that found in water and what they can scrounge from humans—they will also prey on smaller livestock like chickens, ducks, and geese, and stray pets, including small dogs and cats.

1   thl-am-eeg-in uh do-wer

TWRCH TRWYTH
Trwyth's Boar

A gigantic pale boar, with long curling tusks and thick coarse fur which tapers into sharp needles, Twrch Trwyth[1] is a ferocious beast that struck fear into the hearts of those brave, or foolish, enough to try and hunt him down.

Originally an Irish prince, Twrch Trwyth was cursed and turned into a gigantic boar with poisonous bristles for his wickedness. Hidden in the fur between his ears are a pair of scissors, a comb, and a razor. He is accompanied by seven young piglets, all of whom were once men and were close to him; they too had been transformed.

Twrch Trwyth is mentioned in the *Red Book of Hergest* of the *Mabinogion*. This account comes from the story of Culhwch and Olwen, the first written record of Arthurian legend; he is said to have been pursued by King Arthur himself with the help of his loyal dog Cafall.[2] Twrch Trwyth was finally driven to his death into the sea off the Cornish coast.

1   too-er-kh troo-ith
2   kav-athl

TYLWYTH TEG
fair folk

TYLWYTH TEG
fair folk

Tylwyth teg[1] also known as Bendith y Mamau[2] or Blessing of the Mothers, is a collective term for fair folk or fairies in Welsh and Irish mythology.

Fair folk are divided into five classes:
- Bwbachod, or house fairies
- Coblynau, or mine fairies
- Ellyllon, or elves
- Gwragedd Annwn, or water fairies
- Gwyllion, or mountain fairies

According to legend, fairies have a habit of taking kind-hearted babies and young children from their cribs and replacing them with a plentyn newid,[3] or changeling. These changelings would look identical to the child but cause much distress to the parents by screaming, consuming as much food as a full-grown adult, and generally making the parents' lives unpleasant.

The tylwyth teg are sometimes described as hideously ugly, warped in appearance, and deformed. They will sometimes ride a ceffyl dŵr, raiding homes and villages in search of food. This led to many Welsh people leaving bowls of milk outside their homes in order to appease them.

Many people would keep an iron or silver knife on their person, in case they were attacked or cornered by any fair folk. Iron and silver are said to inflict severe burning upon these creatures and brandishing such a weapon will often send them running.

1   terl-with taig
2   ben-deeth uh mam-eye
3   plen-tin nay-weed

BWBACHOD
House Fairies

A bwbach[1] is a type of Welsh house-goblin thought to be a cousin of the English brownie and hobgoblin. Its name derives from the alternate Welsh word for scarecrow, likely due to this creature's appetite for corvids.

These small creatures rarely exceed more than three feet in height; their thick, leathery skin is normally black, brown, or green in colour; they have long, dextrous fingers; and they sport a thick mane of spiny, messy hair on top of their heads and down their backs. Like cats, the bwbachod[2] have a superior ability to see in the dark due to an increased number of light-sensitive rods in their retinas; this gives them a rather frightening appearance should their eyes catch the light.

Many Welsh homes are home to at least one bwbach. They are intelligent little creatures and like to watch their human hosts closely in order to learn new skills.

Bwbachod are quite happy to exchange living in a home for household chores and are impeccably clean creatures; they will sweep floors and clean surfaces in exchange for milk or cream left in a bowl by the fireplace overnight.

Should one of these creatures be spotted scampering about, take care never to approach or speak to it (or any of the fair folk) directly, as it is considered very rude; rather, a person should announce their presence as if speaking to the air. It is important not to offend these creatures or speak rudely about them as they can quickly become unwelcome guests. They do not take kindly to non-pagan people and will take great pleasure playing tricks in an effort to make Christians leave. Indeed, Christian priests have reported being poked, prodded, and shoved when attempting to pray in a home inhabited by bwbachod.

1   boo-bakh
2   boo-bakh-odd

BWCA
Knocker

A bwca[1] or tommyknocker is a creature recognized by Welsh, Cornish, and even Devon folklore; they are believed to be close cousins of the Irish leprechaun and the English brownie. Their legend is widespread and tales of tommyknockers have even been recorded as far away as the United States.

These mischievous humanoid creatures often reside in caves and wells. They are normally around two feet in height, with large ears and mouths, pointed teeth, twinkling eyes, and crooked features. They are mostly hairless but have long white whiskers like a cat sprouting from their eyebrows and chin. Bwcaod[2] take a lot of pride in their appearance and have been known to adorn themselves with clothing, shiny jewellery, and bones that they find lying around.

Bwcaod earned the nickname "knockers" or "tommyknockers" from their habit of knocking on walls to warn miners away from their underground homes. Many believed that they were in fact helpful creatures and would cast some of their food aside to thank them for the warnings and for not attacking them. Unfortunately, these warnings were rarely heeded and some would take to stealing miners' tools and even start chipping away at the supporting timbers, causing the tunnels to give way.

1   boo-ka

2   boo-ka-odd

CEWRI

Giants

In Welsh mythology, the cewri[1] are described as gigantic humanoid creatures, varying between eight and ten feet in height. The males often sport a very long, thick beard, which, sadly, was often kept as a trophy by giant-slayers and fashioned into items of clothing. Cewri are sometimes described as shape-shifters, taking on smaller, more humanoid forms in order to fit into human society.

Not much is known about the cewri culture and the stories vary greatly regarding their behaviour. Within the pages of the *Mabinogion* it is told that once Britain was ruled by a cawr[2] named Bran, who was said to be so tall in his human form that he was unable to stand up straight within any building. There was a monstrous cawr that once terrorized a village close to Craig y Ddinas,[3] stealing livestock and eating small children.

Another legend tells of Idris Gawr, a famous giant warrior and skilled poet, said to be so large that he carved out a gigantic throne for himself in a mountain ridge. Cadair Idris[4] literally translates to "Chair of Idris" and the area is steeped in legend: it is considered to be the mythical hunting grounds of Gwyn ap Nudd,[5] Lord of the Annwn and his red-eared hounds, and is also sometimes called King Arthur's Throne. It is also said that if a person should wander up the mountain alone and stay there after dark, they will either come back mad or a poet.

1   koo-ree
2   kah-ooer
3   kraig uh deen-ahs
4   kad-aye-er eed-rees
5   gw-in ap neeth

COBLYNAU
Mine Fairies

Coblynau[1] are a type of fairy that live deep under the earth, in mountain caves and freshwater wells. They have incredibly large glowing eyes and enormous bat-like ears that help them navigate the deep underground caverns where they live. Their features can give them a somewhat cute appearance, but do not let that fool you as they have a particularly nasty bite. Their mouths are filled with rows of sharp, pointed teeth and their small, furry bodies sport a mane of razor-sharp spines.

Coblynau are fairly bipedal in appearance, and when standing, they can reach roughly a foot and a half in height. Their slim cat-like bodies are perfect for squeezing and contorting through narrow openings and cracks in cave walls.

They are not overly fond of miners. Coblynau mothers are very protective and should a miner stray too close to an underground nest, where the young are kept, coblynau are known to extinguish a miner's lantern and attack.

Coblynau have been known to commit acts of mischief by stealing miners' tools and food and are often held responsible for cave-ins and rock slides. They are especially fond of canaries and will swarm anyone holding one like a school of tiny piranhas just to get a taste. When they are particularly hungry, they have even been known to eat the odd pony or human.

1   cob-learn-eye

ELLYLLON
Elves

Unlike their English and Nordic cousins, the Welsh elves, or ellyllon[1] are considerably shorter than average, only reaching five feet in height.

Contrary to some tales that describe Welsh elves as simply hideous and frightening in appearance, ellyllon are actually incredibly beautiful creatures of supernatural speed and strength, with slim, muscular builds, large bright blue or green eyes, dark skin, pointed ears, and imp-like features. They are remarkably intelligent, and are expert crafters, musicians, hunters, gatherers, and navigators of the forests. Their movements are agile and cat-like as they climb and jump through the trees with ease. They build their homes in hidden woodland groves and deep valleys, as they mostly prefer to keep to themselves, avoiding contact with humans.

They normally sport a mane of thick, curly hair, which is often kept long and styled into thick twists and adorned with beautiful handcrafted beads and jewellery. Their long, pointed ears are usually pierced with golden hoops or carved animal bone.

1   eh-thl-ugh-thl-on

GWRAGEDD ANNWN
Water Fairies

A race of elf-like water fairies that dwell in freshwater lakes and streams, the gwragedd Annwn[1] are often described as pale-skinned humanoids, although their true appearance is quite remarkable: their bodies are covered in green and blue iridescent scales, and they have long, brightly coloured hair, and bright white eyes. In their more human-like form they often appear to be wet and dripping, leaving puddles wherever they walk.

Gwragedd Annwn are very friendly and good-natured creatures. Unlike many fairies they are quite fond of humans, often choosing to live on the outskirts of human towns and happily marrying into human families.

They are remarkably skilled healers held in high regard by many people and often taking up the role of local doctor or surgeon. Their good natures should not be mistaken for weakness; they are a proud people and should a human treat them badly they will cut all ties with that person, never to be seen by them again.

1   goo-rag-aythe an-oon

THE PHYSICIANS OF MYDDFAI:

One tale recounts that during the twelfth century near Llanddeusant,[1] Carmarthenshire, there lived a widow and her son. Every day the son cared for their herd of cattle on the Black Mountain. One day, he came across a beautiful woman sitting by the lake combing her bright green hair. He was overwhelmed by her beauty and offered her some of his bread. She refused and explained that the bread was too tough for her to eat and then wandered back into the lake, disappearing beneath the water.

Upon returning home, the son told his mother what had happened and she advised him that he should offer the woman some bread dough if he should see her again the next day. Sure enough, the beautiful woman was again combing her hair at the side of the lake, so the young man offered her some of the bread dough. She refused yet again, saying it was far too soft and obviously uncooked before disappearing once more beneath the surface. The young son spent all night baking the perfect lightly baked loaf and took it with him the following day. This time the woman accepted and he asked her to marry him. She agreed but clearly explained that should he ever strike her she would leave him and he would never see her again.

The couple lived happily for many years on a farm near the village of Myddfai.[2] They had three sons together who were all healthy and content. However, the wife's behaviour was considered peculiar by the local people; she was not accustomed to human behaviours and acted strangely at social gatherings. On two occasions she started laughing at a funeral and another time she started to weep uncontrollably at a wedding; with everyone staring at them the embarrassed husband struck his wife hard to silence her. Upon being struck her laughter stopped and she silently walked away back up into the hills and disappeared beneath the waters of her lake. He never saw her again.

Her sons, however, visited the lake regularly and she would reunite with them as long as their father wasn't present. She taught them about their fairy heritage and the arts of healing, and her sons went on to become some of the greatest doctors in the land, becoming known as the Physicians of Myddfai.

1   thlan-thre-sant

2   mehr-th-faye

GWYLLION

Mountain Fairies

Gwyllion[1] are fair folk that live high in the Welsh mountains. They are secretive beings and do not appreciate humans wandering into their lands; they will guard lonely Welsh mountain roads and attempt to frighten away anyone that strays too close to their territory.

Like many fair folk, rather than attacking directly, gwyllion have the ability to shape-shift and conjure up apparitions to frighten people or gently lead them astray. They are strongly associated with sheep and goats, and often shape-shift into these creatures in an attempt to hide from human eyes.

Gwyllion are often described as being hideous old women, comparable to hags and witches. But this is a rather unfair description. They are actually a proud race of matriarchal fairy warriors. Their natural forms are humanoid in shape, but they have long, curling horns and soft, floppy ears. Like many fair folk, the gwyllion are allergic to iron. It burns their skin if it touches them, and so lone travellers are strongly advised to carry a knife made from iron to defend themselves against an attack.

Although most gwyllion despise humans, there have been reports of some making their way down from the mountains during especially stormy weather and settling into human inns and even homes for the night, placing themselves close to the fire to enjoy the warmth. It is important to be especially careful and respectful should this happen, by providing your guest with a bowl of clean, freshwater, and removing any iron and knives from the area, as this will cause offence. If these fair folk are treated with respect, they are likely to let locals pass through their mountain homes unharmed.

1   gwee-thl-ee-on

MORGEN
Mermaids

Morgen or mari-morgans[1] are a type of mermaid that lures and drowns unsuspecting travellers to their deaths with their hypnotic beauty. They also have an incredible ability to manipulate water and are often blamed for heavy flooding and rain.

There are reports of morgen living in both fresh water and salt water. They are described as eternally young and are fairly androgynous in appearance. They are often depicted as having a mermaid-like tail, though it seems these creatures can also shape-shift and take on a more humanoid form, depending on what may be more pleasing to the individual they are looking to lure to a watery death.

Like many fair folk they have a habit of letting humans raise their young, often leaving their babies for fishermen to find and raise as their own; once the child reaches adulthood they return to the underwater family and are never seen again.

Their underwater villages are a true sight to behold; their buildings are decorated with jewels, seashells, gold coins, and crystals and their spectacular underwater gardens are filled with colourful corals.

1   marry-morgans

PWCA

Shape-shifters

Most fair folk have the ability to alter their appearance at will; however, the pwca,[1] or pooka in Irish folklore, is particularly talented when it comes to shape-shifting. Often taking on the appearance of wild animals, livestock, and even humans, they can also mimic animal calls and human speech.

Their true form is rarely seen but they are often described as small and animal-like with bright red eyes, covered with a thick layer of either bright white or deep black fur. When transformed into an animal, they will retain their bright white or black coat and striking red eyes.

Pwcaod[2] are renowned tricksters, taking great joy in teaching humans much-needed life lessons, often transforming into animals to give humans a fright. Pwcaod can also be incredibly kind and helpful towards humans, rewarding good and hard-working people with gifts and good fortune.

Long ago, pwcaod and humans lived happily alongside each other, and sightings of them were fairly common. Locals would try to establish good relationships with these creatures by leaving overripe food out and leaving some of their harvests in the fields for them to eat. Sadly, in recent years their numbers have dwindled and sightings have become almost non-existent. Perhaps they went extinct or took on their animal and human forms permanently in order to fit into a more human-populated environment.

1   pooh-ka

2   pooh-ka-odd

YSBRYDION

Spirits

ADERYN Y FAENOL
The Bird of Faenol

The legend of Aderyn y Faenol[1] tells of an ethereal humanoid with a bird-like aspect that is associated with the Faenol Estate, situated in Bangor, North Wales. Dating back to the Tudor period, the estate is nearly one thousand acres, includes over thirty listed buildings within the grounds, and is surrounded by a seven-mile-long wall which encompasses the entire property. This creature is said to be the spirit of a man who was executed for illegally felling trees on the estate and stealing wood. At night the bird perches in the trees shouting "Gwae! Gwae i mi am fenybru fy mwyell a gwympodd y coed y Faenol!" ("Woe! Woe's me, that I ever put a handle to my axe to fell the trees of Faenol!").

Today the area is renowned as a festival venue, which hosts the national Eisteddfod, BBC Radio 1's Big Weekend, and the Bryn Terfels Faenol festival.

ANGELYSTOR
Angel of Death

In Llangernyw[1] village, Conwy, stands St. Digan's Church. The church is centuries old, but the ground it stands on was once sacred pagan land. The churchyard is also home to a pair of standing stones, believed to be a portal to the Celtic Otherworld.

According to local legend, the grounds are home to an ancient Ysbryd,[2] or spirit, known as Angelystor.[3] Each year on Halloween, Angelystor appears between the stones and makes his way to the church altar, where, with a booming voice, he announces the names of those who will die that year.

THE HALLOWEEN PROPHECY:

Legend also tells of a tailor called Siôn ap Robert,[4] who laughed at the idea such a creature existed. One night, while drinking at his local pub, his friends challenged him to visit the church grounds and prove the story was not true. Siôn made his way to the church and explored the grounds; all was still, not a breath of wind shook the trees. After giving up his search, he made his way up to the church door, but as he reached for the door handle a deep voice shook the earth, reciting the names of those who were to die that year, the first of which was Siôn ap Robert. "Hold, hold!" he cried, "I am not ready to die yet!" But, ready or not, he died later that year.

1   thlan-gare-new
2   ugh-sbreed
3   ang-el-er-store

74   4   sean ap robert

CYHYRAETH
Banshee

Cyhyraeth,[1] similar to the Irish banshee and the Scottish ceilleach, is a tormented spirit or wraith with a moaning song that sounds before a person dies.

Cyhyraethau[2] are often sighted or heard before shipwrecks along the Welsh coast and before natural disasters like wildfires and landslides. The cry of the cyhyraeth is also believed to lament Welsh natives who lie dying far from home. Their appearance is often accompanied by balls of light, also known as will-o'-the-wisps or corpse lights, that will often signal the presence of a spirit before it takes on a more solid form. Cyhyraethau have an affinity for water and it is said that long ago they were worshipped as goddesses by the ancient Britons.

Their moaning song can apparently be heard along the coast of Glamorganshire and around the River Tywi[3] in eastern Dyfed.[4] Be warned, however, as sometimes it is said that their moaning can only be heard by those who are about to die.

1   keh-her-eye-th
2   keh-her-eye-th-aye
3   ter-wee
4   duh-ved

Y DYN GWYRDD
The Green Man

Y Dyn Gwyrdd,[1] or the green man, can be found carved into many churches and cathedrals across Britain. However, he has also been observed in many cultures from around the globe spanning numerous ages.

His face is often humanoid and surrounded with leaves, branches, and vines, which can sometimes be seen sprouting from his nose and mouth. Sometimes the shoots will bear flowers and fruit and occasionally small animals and insects can be seen crawling through his leaves.

Primarily he is seen as a symbol of rebirth, representing the growth of plants each spring and is often associated with the worship of trees. This is hardly surprising considering much of Europe was once covered in vast, dense forests and tree worship predated many religious orders. Often, he is viewed as another representation of the horned Celtic god Cernunnos,[2] the Greek nature spirit Pan, or a male counterpart to the Earth goddess, Gaia. The origins of the green man to this day are shrouded in mystery.

1   uh deen goo-earth

78   2   keh-rn-in-nos

GWRACH Y RHIBYN
Hag of the Mist

According to Welsh legend, there is another foreteller of death known as Gwrach y Rhibyn.[1] She is a monstrous spirit who takes the shape of an elderly woman with bird-like features, huge leathery wings, long black teeth, glassy glowing eyes, and pale, sunken features.

Some say she is a cyhyraeth, while others say that she is a water goddess tormented by the loss of her home and has become a monster warped by grief. As with many female spirits and godesses of the time, her legend was demonized and rewritten by the Church throughout the Middle Ages, so little information regarding her original form remains.

As with most Welsh spirits, Gwrach y Rhibyn's presence is often signalled by a ball of light, akin to a candle flame that drifts between houses in the dead of night. She is often spotted during the full moon at crossroads and beside rivers and secluded pools in foggy forested areas.

Similar to the cyhyraeth, Gwrach y Rhibyn is believed to be a harbinger of death and will approach the window of an individual who is soon to die and whisper their name. She is also known to stalk people, appearing several times in the weeks before a person dies. She sings in a voice so soft that only the person about to die can hear her, her voice becoming louder and clearer as they come closer to the end.

It is also believed that Gwrach y Rhibyn would attack people in the night and some tales go as far as to suggest she was especially fond of the blood of young children, the frail, and the elderly who found it difficult to defend themselves. It is said she would drink their blood while they slept, leaving them to slowly waste away from an unknown disease. If a child wasn't growing as they should and was sickly, it was common to place blame upon Gwrach y Rhibyn.

1   goor-akh uh reeb-een

MARI LWYD
Mary White

The Mari Lwyd[1] is not so much a mythical beast, but a human dressed up as a fanciful creature, akin to a puppet, adorned in a white sheet carrying a decorated horse skull, antlers, and holly. This strange Welsh custom is believed to have originated in the regions of Glamorgan and Gwent. It is unique to the South of Wales and used to mark the passing of the darkest days of mid-winter.

The puppet-costume consists of a horse's skull decorated with ribbons fixed to a pole. A white sheet is attached to the back of the skull, which drapes down to conceal both the pole and the individual. In some instances, the horse's jaw is able to open and close as a result of string or lever. It can still be seen parading the streets at Llangynwyd,[2] near Maesteg,[3] every New Year's Day. People taking part call at local houses and sing songs to gain entry; the homeowner is expected to deny entry at first, before relenting and inviting everyone in for food and drink.

The tradition of the Mari Lwyd has ancient pre-Christian origins. In Celtic Britain, the horse was believed to be a symbol of power, fertility, and prowess on the battlefield. Many believed these animals had the ability to cross between this world and the Otherworld and mid-winter is a time when the veil between worlds is especially thin.

1	marry loo-ede
2	thlan-gun-wid
3	mice-teg

ABOUT THE AUTHOR

C.C.J. Ellis

Born in April 1989, Collette June Ellis grew up in Bangor, surrounded by the spectacular landscapes of North Wales. Ellis' work is often inspired by fantasy and mythology, drawing inspiration from ancient cultures from around the world. *The Hobbit* by J.R.R.Tolkien was one of their favourite books as a child and they later fell in love with the artwork involved in *The Lord of the Rings* movies and the work of Japanese film director Hayao Miyazaki.

Ellis attended Glyndŵr University in Wrexham and achieved a Master's degree in Design Communication. During their studies, they travelled to China after being awarded a grant by the Welsh Livery Guild to investigate dragon legends in both countries. In 2017 they were lucky to receive another grant from the Welsh government to return to China to gather more information for future art books.

They have exhibited at various conventions across the United Kingdom; including London MCM Comic Con and Thought Bubble UK. In October 2016 they opened their third solo exhibition in the Oriel Yuys Môn[1] (The Anglesey Gallery), and they have launched a number of successful crowdfunding campaigns.

In the past, Ellis has been featured in several online blogs and magazines, including *ImagineFX* magazine. They have appeared on *Y Lle*[2] on Welsh TV channel S4C and BBC's *Wales Today* show, and taken part in a one-to-one art podcast with *Pencil Kings*.

1   oriel un-is mourn

2   uh thlee

SPECIAL THANKS
TO EVERYONE INVOLVED

Foreword

Stephanie Law

www.shadowscapes.com

Sian Powell

www.celticmythspodcast.com

Appraisal

Todd Lockwood

www.toddlockwood.com

John Howe

www.john-howe.com

Publisher

Eye of Newt Books

www.eyeofnewtpress.com

Headshot

Jody Kite

www.jodykite.photography.com

Graphic Design

Fleur Ellis

www.fleurellis.co.uk

Iris Compiet

www.iriscompiet.art

Eye of Newt Books

www.eyeofnewtpress.com

Welsh Translation

Alun Gruffydd

www.bla-translation.co.uk

Rhyn Williams

WOOL of BAT

a imprint from

EYE of NEWT
BOOKS